ONE OF THE PROBLEMS OF
Everett Anderson

ONE OF THE PROBLEMS OF
Everett Anderson

Lucille Clifton

ILLUSTRATIONS BY
Ann Grifalconi

HENRY HOLT AND COMPANY · NEW YORK

Henry Holt and Company, LLC
Publishers since 1866
115 West 18th Street, New York, New York 10011

Henry Holt is a registered trademark of Henry Holt and Company, LLC
Text copyright © 2001 by Lucille Clifton
Illustrations copyright © 2001 by Ann Grifalconi
All rights reserved.
Published in Canada by Fitzhenry & Whiteside Ltd.,
195 Allstate Parkway, Markham, Ontario L3R 4T8.

Library of Congress Cataloging-in-Publication Data
Clifton, Lucille. One of the problems of Everett Anderson / by Lucille Clifton; illustrations by Ann Grifalconi.
Summary: Everett Anderson wonders how he can help his friend Greg, who appears to be a victim of child abuse.
[1. Child abuse—Fiction. 2. Afro-Americans—Fiction. 3. Stories in rhyme.] I. Grifalconi, Ann, ill. II. Title.
PZ8.3.C573 On 2001   [E]—dc21   00-57514
ISBN 0-8050-5201-1 / First Edition—2001 / Designed by Donna Mark
Printed in the United States of America on acid-free paper. ∞

1 3 5 7 9 10 8 6 4 2

To all those who need a friend, speak!

—L. C. and A. G.

Everett Anderson sits at home
wondering what he should say
or do.

A room can be lonely
when a boy, not grown,
every day sees his new friend Greg
with a scar or a bruise mark on his leg.

"Maybe he really falls down stairs,
but every day could he be stumbling
and nobody ever notices Greg
being clumsy or slipping or tumbling?"

"Well, it's none of our business." Evelyn sighs.
"But we're friends," pouts Everett.
"He's one of the guys."

When Mama looks in, she wants to know
what is upsetting her children so.

"One day in school, just out of the blue,"
Everett whispers, "Greg started to cry,
and I went over to ask him why,
and he looked up and sighed,
'I can't tell you.'

"And he had the saddest, saddest face,
like he was lost in the loneliest place.

"I could tell the teacher,
but I'm afraid
in case he asks me what I mean
and I don't know exactly,

it might seem
stupid or some mistake I've made,
and I don't want to make it bad
for Greg or for his mom and dad."

Mama sits with her children a while
and hugs them hard
and holds Everett's hand,

and Everett tries to understand
that one of the things he can do right now
is listen to Greg and hug and hold
his friend, and now that Mama is told,
something will happen for Greg that is new.

Sometimes the little things you do
make a difference.
Everett Anderson hopes that's true.